SQUEAK-A-LOT

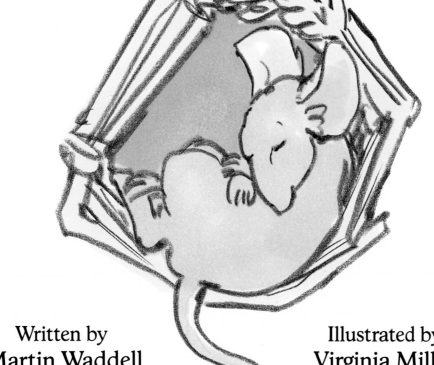

Written by
Martin Waddell

Illustrated by
Virginia Miller

WALKER BOOKS
AND SUBSIDIARIES
LONDON • BOSTON • SYDNEY

In an old old house lived a small small mouse
who had no one to play with.

THIS WALKER BOOK BELONGS TO:

_____

_____

_____

_____

For Peter
M.W.

For Jane
V.M.

First published 1991 by Walker Books Ltd
87 Vauxhall Walk, London SE11 5HJ

This edition published 1993

6 8 10 9 7

Text © 1991 Martin Waddell
Illustrations © 1991 Virginia Miller

The right of Martin Waddell to be identified as author
of this work has been asserted by him in accordance
with the Copyright, Designs and Patents Act 1988.

Printed in Hong Kong

British Library Cataloguing in Publication Data
A catalogue record for this book is
available from the British Library.

ISBN 0-7445-3047-4

So the small small mouse went out of the house
to find a friend to play with.

And he found
a bee.

"Can I play with you?"
the mouse asked the bee.
"Of course," said the bee.
"What will we play?"
asked the mouse.
"We'll play Buzz-a-lot,"
said the bee.

BUZZ BUZZ BUZZ BUZZ BUZZ!
But the mouse didn't like it a lot.
So he went to find a better friend to play with.

And he found
a dog.

"Can I play with you?"
the mouse asked the dog.
"Of course," said the dog.
"What will we play?"
asked the mouse.
"We'll play Woof-a-lot,"
said the dog.

WOOF WOOF WOOF WOOF!
But the mouse didn't like it a lot.
So he went to find a better friend to play with.

And he found
a chicken.

"Can I play with you?"
the mouse asked the
chicken.
"Of course," said the
chicken.
"What will we play?"
asked the mouse.
"We'll play Cluck-a-lot,"
said the chicken.

CLUCK CLUCK CLUCK CLUCK!
But the mouse didn't like it a lot.
So he went to find a better friend to play with.

And he found a cat.

"Can I play with you?"
the mouse asked the cat. And . . .

WHAM! BAM! SCRAM!
The mouse didn't like it a lot.

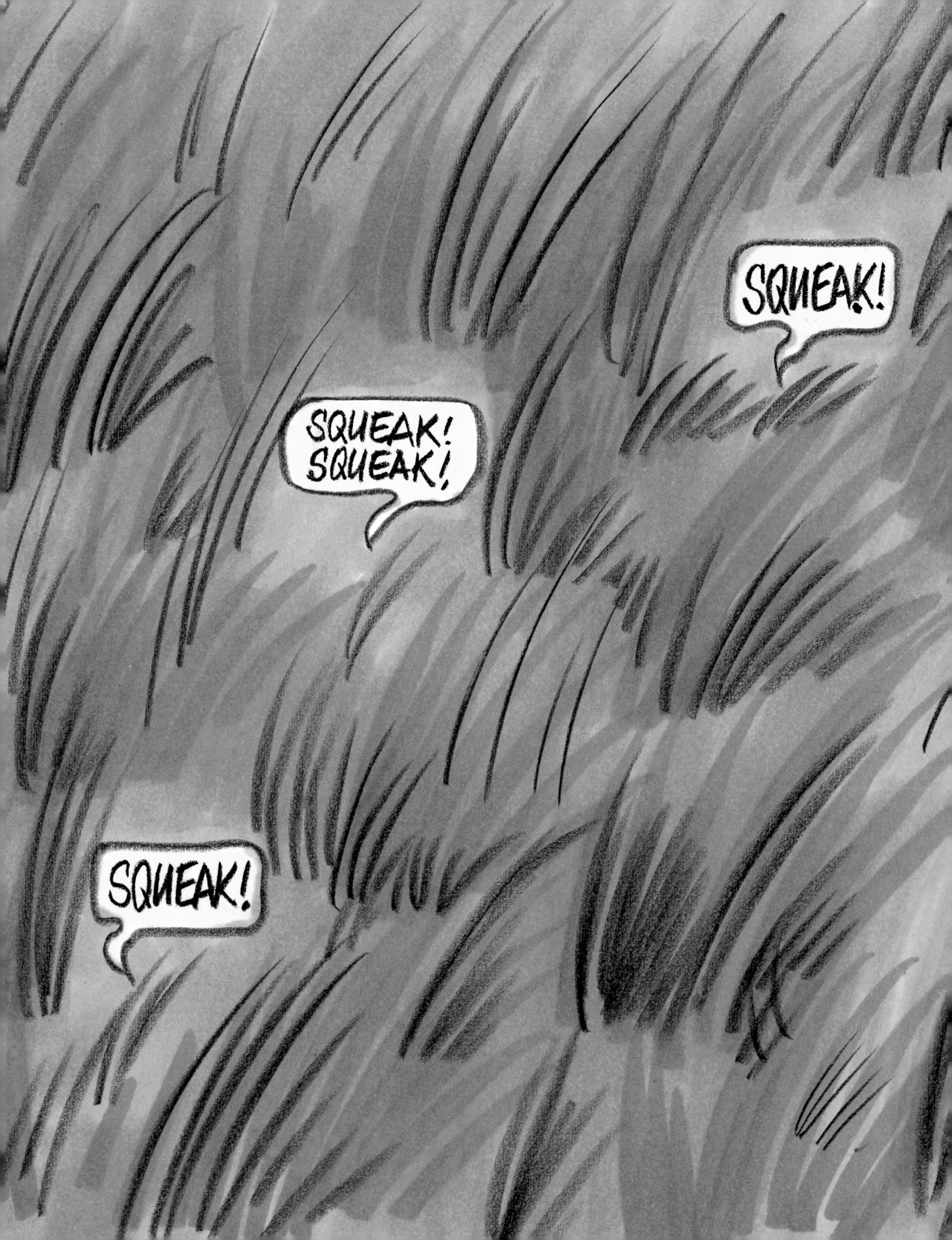
SQUEAK!
SQUEAK! SQUEAK!
SQUEAK!

So he ran away through the long long grass
playing Squeak-a-lot all by himself.
SQUEAK SQUEAK SQUEAK SQUEAK!

SQUEAK! Some mice found the mouse.
"Can we play with you?" the mice asked the mouse.
"Of course," said the mouse.
"What will we play?" asked the mice.

"Buzz-a-lot!" said the mouse. BUZZ BUZZ BUZZ
BUZZ BUZZ BUZZ BUZZ! And all of them liked it a lot.

"Woof-a-lot!" said the mouse. WOOF WOOF WOOF WOOF WOOF WOOF! And all of them liked it a lot.

"Cluck-a-lot!" said the mouse. CLUCK CLUCK CLUCK CLUCK CLUCK! And all of them liked it a lot.

"WHAM! BAM! SCRAM!" said the mouse.

SQUEAK SQUEAK SQUEAK SQUEAK!
The mouse chased the mice through the

long long grass back home to the old old house.
And together they played . . .

Sleep-a-lot.